For my daughters,
Sheena and Breanne

Julia —
Stay off of those Bee's!!
We love you forever and
ever —
Grandma +
Grandpa
Hale

Julia,
You are unique in so many
ways — Always Believe!
M. Wayne Adam

Author's Note

The Little Miss Grubby Toes series is written not only for young children, but for parents as well. While some of the situations are intense, the importance of establishing safeguards and discussing safety rules is clearly stressed. Hopefully this will help prevent injuries and save lives.

Discussion questions for parents and teachers are provided at the end of each story, along with a variety of entertaining and educational activities for children.

Little Miss Grubby Toes' mishaps help youngsters realize the consequences of making bad decisions. While Little Miss Grubby Toes always recovers from her misadventures, her parents and community point out that some children are not always so fortunate. Parents may wish to expand on this at an appropriate level for their children.

This is also a good time to examine the inner voice within each of us. "If it doesn't feel right, it usually isn't." Parents can also stress "Ask us first."

A final note: Little Miss Grubby Toes' mother and father are not negligent parents. They love their daughter very much and have obviously talked to her about specific dangers; rules have been clearly established. But in a single moment of relaxed vigilance, young children can get themselves into dangerous predicaments. In reading these stories, parents can examine ways to ingrain household and safety rules, how to implement preventive safety measures, and reflect upon their own supervision.

Other Books by Eddie Price

Eddie Price's historical novel, *Widder's Landing*, now in its fourth printing, has won numerous awards, including the U.S. Daughters of 1812's *Spirit of 1812 Award*, the Gold Medal for Best Historical Fiction at the 2013 Readers' Favorite Awards, and inclusion in the 2014 Kentucky State Fair's Special Exhibitions Bibliography.

Little Miss Grubby Toes

written by
Eddie Price

illustrated by
Mark Wayne Adams

Steps on a Bee

Published by:

Contact Information:
Mark Wayne Adams, Inc.
Attn.: Mark Wayne Adams
PO Box 916392
Longwood, FL 32791

www.mwa.company

Author: Eddie Price
Illustrator/Designer: Mark Wayne Adams
Editor: Jennifer Thomas

Eddie Price
First Edition

Library of Congress Control Number: 2015934994
ISBN-13: 978-1-59616-026-2
ISBN-10: 1-59616-026-8

First Printing 2015
Published in the United States of America
Printed in Canada

Once there was a little girl named Little Miss Grubby Toes. That was not her real name, of course! That was the nickname her father gave her.

Why do you think he called her that?

1

It was because Little Miss Grubby Toes never wore her shoes! Whenever she went outside, she took them off and ran around barefoot.

She walked on blacktop parking lots, tramped through the neighbor's flowerbed, and even shuffled across the gravel driveway! All without her shoes. She loved to squish her toes in the mud after a rain.

Little Miss Grubby Toes' feet—and especially her toes—were grubby all the time!

Now, *usually* Little Miss Grubby Toes was a good little girl.

But sometimes Little Miss Grubby Toes didn't obey her parents. And this *always* got her into trouble.

One day Little Miss Grubby Toes wanted to go out and play. It was such a lovely summer day. The sun was shining. The birds were singing. The bees were buzzing.

"Mother, may I go outside to play?" Little Miss Grubby Toes asked.

"Yes, you may, sweetheart. But you must promise me that you will keep your shoes on today. You must not play barefoot."

"Why not, Mother?"

"Because, Little Miss Grubby Toes, your father has not mowed the yard lately. So there are bees buzzing around the wildflowers."

5

"What are bees, Mother?" asked Little Miss Grubby Toes.

"Bees are a type of insect," Mother told her. "They are yellow and black, and they have three pairs of legs and two pairs of wings. Some bees suck up nectar from flowers and take it to their homes to make honey. They are called honeybees."

"What is nectar?" asked Little Miss Grubby Toes.

"It is a sweet liquid found inside flowers," Mother said. "It is what's used to make the good honey that we eat."

"May I pet the bees?" Little Miss Grubby Toes asked.

"Oh no!" said Mother. "They will hurt you. Their sharp stingers will stick you, especially if you step on them with your bare feet. That is why I want you to wear your shoes today. Do not take them off."

"I promise, Mother!" said Little Miss Grubby Toes.

"Then you may go outside and play."

Little Miss Grubby Toes was happy to be outside.

She liked to swing. She liked to go down the slide.

Most of all, Little Miss Grubby Toes liked to run! She chased the neighbor's kitty, but it ran away. She chased a robin and tried to catch a butterfly. They both flew away.

Soon, Little Miss Grubby Toes was tired. And Little Miss Grubby Toes was hot.

Little Miss Grubby Toes wanted to take off her shoes.

She looked up at the open kitchen window. Mother was not there. Little Miss Grubby Toes could hear Mother talking on the telephone in the other room.

Little Miss Grubby Toes' feet were burning up.

Should she take off her shoes?

NO!
Don't do it!
Listen to your mother!
Watch out for the bees!

14

15

But she did.

The mud at the bottom of the slide felt so nice and cool on Little Miss Grubby Toes' feet. And she didn't see any bees nearby. Maybe if she stayed close to the play area, everything would be alright.

Suddenly, Little Miss Grubby Toes saw a beautiful yellow butterfly flutter past her swing. She wanted so badly to catch it.

18

She leapt off the swing and ran! She forgot all about her bare feet.
She forgot what Mother had told her about the bees.

Oh no!

Little Miss Grubby
Toes stepped on a bee!

The bee's sharp stinger went straight into the bottom of Little Miss Grubby Toes' foot. It *really* hurt!

"Ow-w-w-w!"

screamed Little Miss Grubby Toes.

Then she began to cry.

Mother ran out to help her. Little Miss
Grubby Toes cried and cried!

Mother carried Little Miss Grubby Toes into the house and set her in a kitchen chair.

Without speaking, she examined Little Miss Grubby Toes' foot and gently pulled out the bee's stinger. Then she washed both feet with warm, soapy water and put some medicine and a bandage on the bee sting.

Mother held Little Miss Grubby Toes in her arms until she stopped crying.

When Father came home from work, he knew something was wrong.

"What happened to my Little Miss Grubby Toes?" he asked.

"I told her she could play outside if she wore her shoes," Mother explained. "But she did not obey me and she stepped on a bee!"

"Let me see!" Father said. He peeled back the bandage and looked at the big bump on the bottom of Little Miss Grubby Toes' foot.

"I'll bet that hurts!" he said.

"It does, Father," said Little Miss Grubby Toes, her eyes welling with tears again.

"And *why* did the bee sting you?"

"Because I stepped on it when I was not wearing my shoes," said Little Miss Grubby Toes. "Even though Mother told me to." She sniffled.

Father hugged her. "So what did you learn today, Little Miss Grubby Toes?"

She thought about that for a while.

Then she answered: "I should always listen to my mother. Mother knows what is best and she loves me. You do, too!"

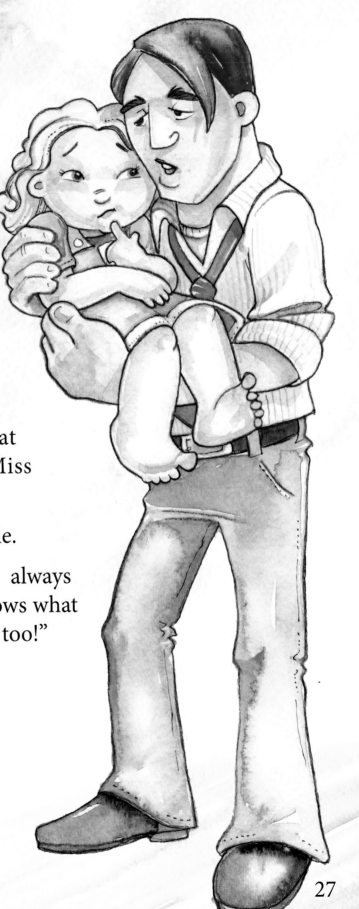

That night, Little Miss Grubby Toes ate all of her supper, so Mother gave her a bowl of ice cream for dessert.

Father said that the bee sting would itch for a few days and that it might be hard to walk on the big bump.

"Some boys and girls," he told her, "get very sick when they are stung by a bee. Some must even go to the hospital to get well."

But Little Miss Grubby Toes was lucky. All she got was a big, itchy bump.

Little Miss Grubby Toes *felt* lucky, too. The ice cream with chocolate sauce was delicious!

That night, she promised to be good forever.

Do you think she will?

Would you like to know Little Miss Grubby Toes' real name?

Here's a hint to the first letter:

What do you do with your eyes?

What letter of the alphabet does that sound like?

Did you get it right? Stay tuned for Little Miss Grubby Toes' next adventure to find out and get another clue to her real name!

Don't miss the next book in the *Little Miss Grubby Toes Series:*

Little Miss Grubby Toes Plays with Fire!

Little Miss Grubby Toes is excited when her friend's birthday cake candles are lit! Her parents warn her not to play with matches, but Little Miss Grubby Toes doesn't listen. What do you think will happen?

Quiz

1. What does a bee look like?

2. Why do bees like flowers?

3. Why did Mother tell Little Miss Grubby Toes to wear shoes?

4. What happened when Little Miss Grubby Toes stepped on a bee?

5. What did Mother do to help Little Miss Grubby Toes?

6. What happens to someone who is stung by a bee?

7. What did Little Miss Grubby Toes learn from all of this?

BONUS QUESTION: Why do bees have stingers?

Answer Key:
1. Yellow and black, three pairs of legs, two pairs of wings.
2. Bees suck nectar from them to make honey.
3. Because she might step on a bee.
4. The bee stung her—and it hurt!
5. She took out the stinger, washed her foot, and applied medicine and a bandage.
6. Pain, swelling, itching, possible hospital stays.
7. Listen to parents, bees make honey, the dangers of bee stings.
BONUS QUESTION: To defend themselves and their beehive.

Can you find these words in
Little Miss Grubby Toes' story?

Grubby	Bee
Insect	Butterfly
Nectar	Honey
Stinger	Medicine
Bandage	Promise